This book belongs to:

(Humphrey, please don't eat it!)

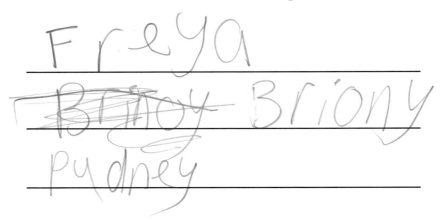

For M, the best storyteller, love - Anna
To my family, with love - Laura

NorthParadePublishing

©2015 North Parade Publishing Ltd.
4 North Parade,
Bath BA1 1LF. UK
www.nppbooks.co.uk

The Big Sad Wolf
The Mean Little Pigs

as told by...

Humphrey Bookworm

Written by Anna Clothier
Illustrated by Laura Wood

northParadePublishing

Max loves stories. Mum's are good, but Humphrey's are **better**.

Humphrey is a bookworm. He lives with Mum, Dad, and Max in **number 71**. He reads all day and eats books for breakfast.

Dad says could he please eat the newspapers instead?
Humphrey says no; they don't fill him up.

Humphrey has been getting fatter and fatter ever since Mum bought a Kindle; now he worries that every meal might be his last...

Every night before bed, Humphrey tells Max a story. He doesn't read it from a book; Humphrey's stories are all in his head.

"Once upon a time, there lived three little pigs..."
begins Humphrey.

"I know that one!" interrupts Max.

"No, you don't!" says Humphrey crossly. "You just think you do.

This is what really happened".

"Once upon a time,

there lived three little pigs and a big sad wolf."

"You mean a **big bad wolf!**" interrupts Max.
"No, I don't!" snapped Humphrey. *"This is what really happened…"*

"Each little pig built
a house for himself:

one of straw,

another
of sticks,

and the third
of bricks.

One day, the big sad wolf came to introduce himself to his new neighbours, for he was very lonely, and hoped to make friends.

The little pig who lived in the house of straw ran inside and locked the door as soon as he saw the wolf approach.

'Little pig, little pig, please let me in!' cried the big sad wolf.

'No!' yelled the mean little pig. 'By the hair of my chinny chin chin, I won't let you in!'

'Please?' cried the big sad wolf. 'I have a terrible cold, and I don't feel well!'

With that, the wolf wheezed, and he sneezed, and completely by accident, he blew the house of straw down!

The mean little pig fled to his brother's house of sticks, and the big sad wolf was lonely and poorly still.

The poor wolf went on to the house of sticks.

He wanted to say: **'Sorry'**

to the first little pig for
sneezing his house down.

The little pig who lived in the house of sticks, and
the little pig who used to live in the house of straw,
both ran inside and locked the door as soon as they
saw the wolf approach.

'Little pigs, little pigs, please let me in!' cried the big sad wolf.

'No!' yelled the mean little pigs. 'By the hair of our chinny chin chins, we won't let you in!'

'Please?' cried the big sad wolf. 'I have a terrible cold, and I don't feel well!'

With that, the big sad wolf wheezed, and he sneezed, and completely by accident, he blew the house of sticks down!

The mean little pigs fled to their brother's house of bricks, and the big sad wolf was lonely and poorly still.

The poor wolf went on to the house of bricks.

He wanted to say sorry to the first and second little pigs for sneezing their houses down, and he still wanted to make friends.

The little pig who lived in the house of bricks, and the little pigs who used to live in the house of straw and the house of sticks, all ran inside and locked the door as soon as they saw the wolf approach.

'Little pigs, little pigs, please let me in!' cried the big sad wolf.

'No!' yelled the mean little pigs. 'By the hair of our chinny chin chins, we won't let you in!'

'Please?' cried the big sad wolf. 'I have a terrible cold, and I don't feel at all well!

With that, the big sad wolf wheezed, and he sneezed, and he wheezed, and he sneezed, but the sturdy little house of bricks did not fall down.

Even so, the mean little pigs would not make friends with the wolf, and he was lonely and poorly still...

The big sad wolf decided he did not want to be friends with such mean little pigs after all, and he left,

wheezing and *sneezing* as he went.

On his way he met another wolf running down the lane, huffing, and puffing, and trying to catch his breath.

'Where are you going?' asked the big sad wolf.

'**I need somewhere to hide!**' panted the second wolf.
'There's been a horrible misunderstanding at Red Riding Hood's
Grandmother's house, and the woodcutter is chasing me!'

'Hide at my house!' suggested the

big-suddenly-not-so-sad wolf

at once, and they set off home together."

Humphrey finishes his story and clears his throat.

"That poor wolf!" cries Max. "He wasn't bad at all; it was all an accident! And those little pigs were so mean to him!"

"There are two sides to every story", says Humphrey wisely.

"But where are all the books that tell his side of the story?" asks Max.

"I ate them!" he said.